www.FlowerpotPress.com
PAB-0808-0284
ISBN: 978-1-4867-1789-7
Made in China/Fabriqué en Chine

# FINN'S FUN TRUCKS
# HEAVY HAULERS

Written by Finn Coyle  Illustrated by Srimalie Bassani

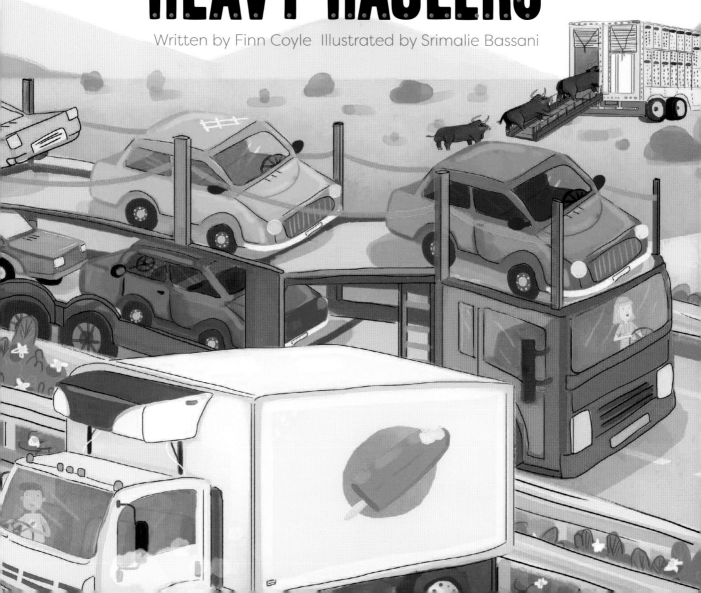

We are the heavy haulers. We move some big loads down the road with the help of our big rigs.

Each one has a different type of trailer used to carry our shipments. Can you guess what each one carries?

This is a
**TANKER.**
Can you guess what it carries?

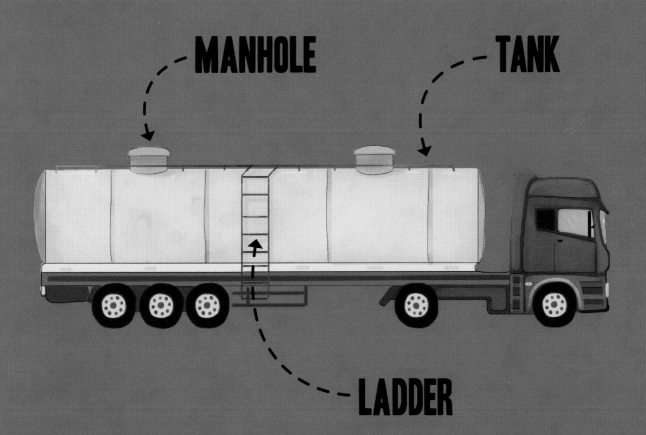

A tanker is used to carry liquids like milk.

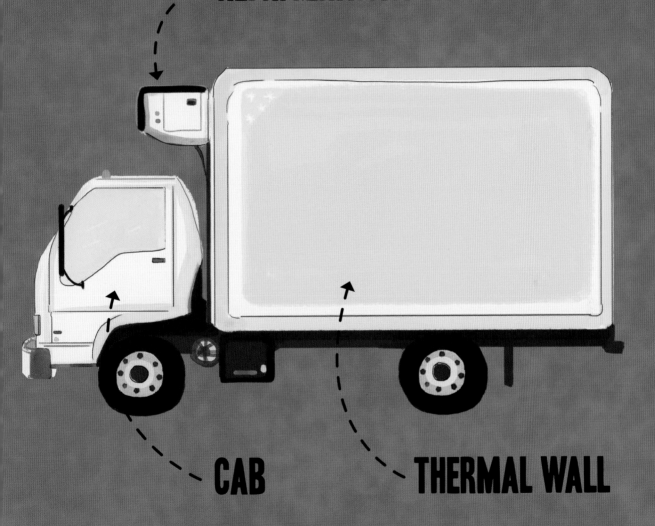

REFRIGERATION UNIT

CAB

THERMAL WALL

A refrigerator truck is used to carry things that need to stay cold like ice cream.

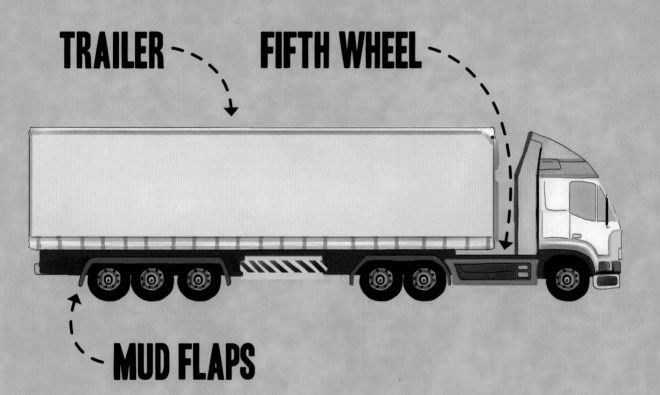

TRAILER

FIFTH WHEEL

MUD FLAPS

A dry van is the most common type of trailer. It is used to carry everyday items like cereal boxes.

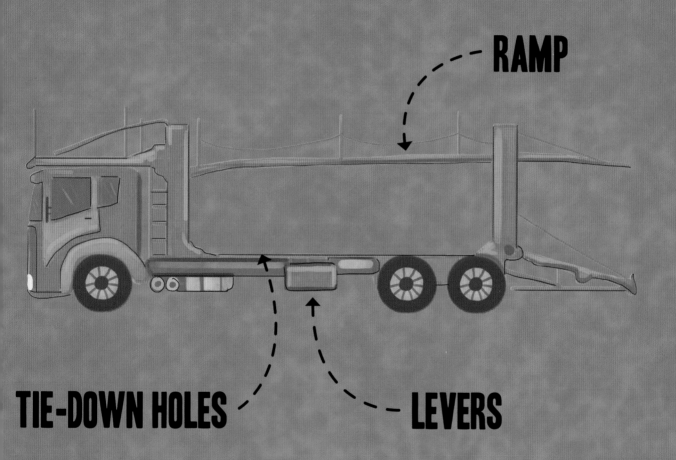

RAMP

TIE-DOWN HOLES

LEVERS

An auto hauler is used to carry cars and trucks.

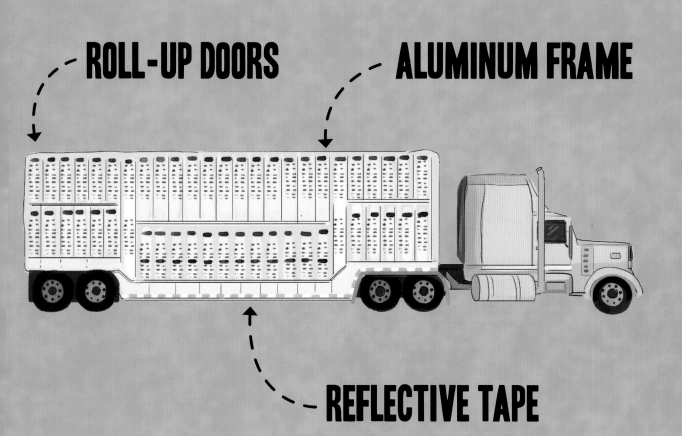

**ROLL-UP DOORS**

**ALUMINUM FRAME**

**REFLECTIVE TAPE**

A bull hauler is used to carry animals.

We are the heavy haulers!

Can you guess what we can do when we all work together?

We can carry lots of things to all the places they need to go!

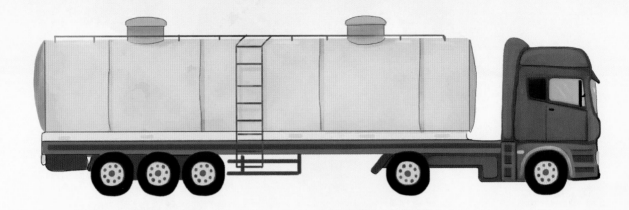

TANKER

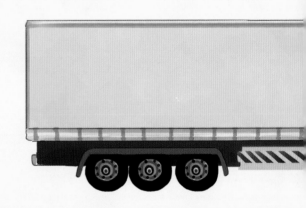

REFRIGERATOR VAN

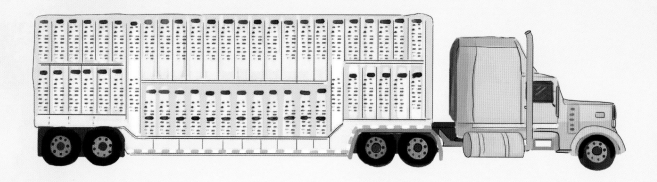

**BULL HAULER**

**DRY VAN**

**AUTO HAULER**